To my son, Adam, and my grandsons, Max and Charlie, who all love the Big Cheese! KH

For Norma, good friend to Angelina and me, with love HC

VIKING
Published by the Penguin Group
Penguin Group (USA) LLC
375 Hudson Street
New York, New York 10014

USA ★ Canada ★ UK ★ Ireland ★ Australia
New Zealand ★ India ★ South Africa ★ China

penguin.com
A Penguin Random House Company

First published in the United States of America by Viking, an imprint of Penguin Young Readers Group, 2014

Text copyright © 2014 by Katharine Holabird
Illustrations copyright © 2014 by Helen Craig Ltd.

LIBRARY OF CONGRESS CATALOGING-IN-PUBLICATION DATA
Holabird, Katharine.
Angelina's big city ballet / by Katharine Holabird; illustrations by Helen Craig.
pages cm.
Angelina goes to the most famous city in Mouseland to perform at the Big Cheese Dance Show with her cousin Jeanie, but the two clash over whether tap or ballet is better.
ISBN 9780670015603 (hardcover)
[1. Dance—Fiction. 2. Competition (Psychology)—Fiction. 3. Cousins—Fiction. 4. Mice—Fiction]
I. Craig, Helen, illustrator. II. Title
PZ7.H689 Amk 2014
[E]
2013000464

Manufactured in China

1   3   5   7   9   10   8   6   4   2

Designed by Eileen Savage

Angelina's Big City Ballet

Story by **Katharine Holabird** Illustrations by **Helen Craig**

VIKING

An Imprint of Penguin Group (USA)

Angelina was on her way to the most famous city in
Mouseland. "Wow! I've always wanted to see
the Big Cheese," she told her friend Captain
Whiskers. Angelina was going to perform at
the Big Cheese Dance Show with her
cousin Jeanie, and she could hardly
wait to get there.

As soon as the S.S. *Mousatania* arrived, Captain Whiskers escorted Angelina down the gangplank to meet Aunt Violet and Cousin Jeanie. Angelina did her best pirouette. "Thank you for inviting me," she said.

"Welcome to the Big Cheese, Angelina," said Aunt Violet. "We're delighted you've come to stay!"

They hopped into a taxi and zoomed through the bustling city. Angelina stared in wonder at all the amazing sights. Glass buildings reached to the sky, buses and taxis roared through the streets, and the sidewalks were packed with busy mice racing wildly in all directions.

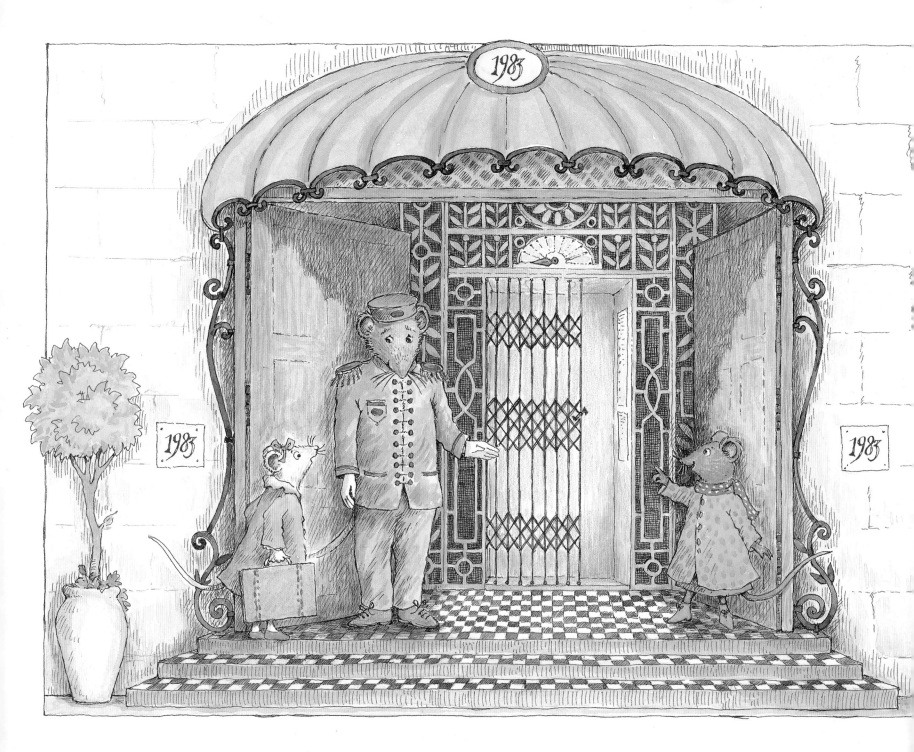

When they got to Aunt Violet's apartment building, Angelina wasn't sure what to do. She'd never seen a doorman or an elevator before.

"Don't be a scaredy mouse!" teased Jeanie, rushing ahead.

Angelina nervously followed Jeanie into the elevator, and it rumbled all the way up to a fancy apartment on the tenth floor.

It was all very different from Angelina's little cottage in Chipping Cheddar!

"Come and see my room," said Jeanie. She proudly showed Angelina all her dance posters and special outfits.

"I'm crazy about tap dancing," Jeanie announced as she danced all around her bedroom. "I'm going to do a special tap dance for the Big Cheese Dance Show. What are you going to do, Angelina?"

"I made up a fairy ballet," said Angelina, practicing her pliés.

"I guess that's OK. . . ." said Jeanie. "But don't you want to try my tap dance? It's much better than ballet."

"Oh," said Angelina, and her tail drooped as she followed her cousin into the kitchen.

The next day, as soon as the mouselings had finished their breakfast, Aunt Violet said, "It's time for our tour of the Big Cheese," and off they went.

The first stop was famous Parmesan Park Avenue, where they visited all the fancy stores filled with beautiful fashions. Aunt Violet loved shopping and bought an enormous hat, while Jeanie danced in front of the mirrors.

Next they went to the Empire Cheddar Building, the highest spot in all of Mouseland. The elevator zoomed up to the hundreth floor, and Angelina felt dizzy. "Imagine tap-dancing way up here," said Jeanie.

As a final treat, Aunt Violet took the mouselings to see the very latest Broadway mousical. It was called *River Mouse* and featured a big chorus line of tap-dancing performers. Jeanie was thrilled. "See! I told you that tap was better than ballet!" she exclaimed.

On the way home, Angelina didn't even feel like twirling.
"Maybe tap is better than ballet after all," she thought.

When she got into bed, Angelina lay worrying about her performance at the Big Cheese Dance Show.

But as soon as she closed her eyes, she started dreaming about dancing. In her dream, Miss Lilly was encouraging her. "Don't give up now, Angelina. The show must go on!"

Angelina woke from her dream with a start. "Miss Lilly's right," she thought. "The show must go on, so I've got to practice my dance!"

She quietly tiptoed out of bed and started to practice her fairy dance in the moonlight.

When Angelina had finished dancing, she curtsied and then looked up. There was Jeanie, clapping in the doorway.

"That was so beautiful!" said Jeanie. "I'm sorry I said tap is better than ballet. My dance isn't as good as yours."

And then Jeanie started to cry. Angelina gave her cousin a hug and said, "Let's help each other—it's much more fun together."

Jeanie wiped her tears away, and then the cousins sat side by side and thought up a wonderful plan.

The next day Angelina and Jeanie started practicing their dance. Angelina showed Jeanie some of her favorite ballet routines, and Jeanie showed Angelina some of her best tap-dancing steps.

"We're making up our own dance," said Jeanie happily.

"We'll call it the Big City Ballet!" said Angelina, doing a little twirl.

Aunt Violet was very pleased with their hard work and gave Angelina and Jeanie special costumes for the show.

At last the big night arrived, and Angelina and Jeanie joined all the other young dancers backstage at the Big Cheese Dance Show. When Angelina saw the beautiful stage lit up with lights, and the eagerly waiting crowds, her tail tingled with excitement.

"Let's welcome Angelina and Jeanie with their Big City Ballet!"
said the presenter, and the mouseling cousins whispered, "Good luck!"
to each other and took a deep breath as they tiptoed up the stairs to the stage.

The two little dancers twirled and tapped together across the stage and performed their special dance like two sparkling stars. Everyone clapped and cheered, and Angelina was happy to see Aunt Violet smiling proudly in the front row.

When the show was over, Angelina and Jeanie hugged each other.
Aunt Violet said, "Well done, my big city dancers!"

For the rest of the trip, Angelina and Jeanie twirled and tapped together all around the Big Cheese. When it was time to go, Jeanie gave Angelina a pair of her shiny tap shoes. "Come back soon so we can dance together again."

"I will," promised Angelina. "I can't wait to do another Big City Ballet!" Angelina gave Jeanie a pair of her best pink ballet slippers, and then she waved good-bye as the S.S. *Mousatania* tooted its horn and set sail for home.